FAST FLIGHT

An **RFDS** Adventure

For Brendan Wells, whose real-life story inspired this fictional tale. – G. I.

A Random House book
Published by Random House Australia Pty Ltd
Level 3, 100 Pacific Highway, North Sydney NSW 2060
www.randomhouse.com.au

Penguin
Random House
Australia

First published by Random House Australia in 2016

Random House Books is part of the Penguin Random House group of companies whose addresses can be found at global.penguinrandomhouse.com/offices.

National Library of Australia
Cataloguing-in-Publication Entry

Author: Ivanoff, George, 1968–
Title: Fast flight
ISBN: 978 0 85798 882 9 (pbk)
Series: Royal Flying Doctor Service; 4
Target Audience: For primary school age
Subjects: Royal Flying Doctor Service of Australia
           Medical emergencies – Juvenile fiction
Dewey number: A823.3

Cover and internal illustrations by Maria Pena
Cover design by Christabella Designs
Internal design and typesetting by Midland Typesetters, Australia
Printed in Australia by Griffin Press, an accredited ISO AS/NZS 14001:2004
Environmental Management System printer

Random House Australia uses papers that are natural, renewable and recyclable products and made from wood grown in sustainable forests. The logging and manufacturing processes are expected to conform to the environmental regulations of the country of origin.

FAST FLIGHT

An **RFDS** Adventure

GEORGE IVANOFF

RANDOM HOUSE AUSTRALIA

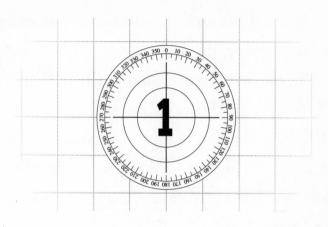

Four years ago . . .

'Dillon squinted into the light. Other-worldly light! He could feel the power flooding over him. Through him. Dillon blazed through time, speeding into the far distant future. As he stepped out of the time-travelling light box, he gazed in awe at the fantastic world around him.'

'What did I see?' asked Dillon, quivering with excitement.

'There were impossibly tall buildings, flying cars and hover shoes,' continued Dad. 'Everyone looked happy. Everyone looked healthy. Because in this future world, there was no illness or disease. The clever doctors had fixed it all.'

Dillon smiled up at his dad. 'I like this story best.'

'I think I do, too,' said Dad. 'I like imagining you as a time traveller.'

'I like imagining a future world with no sickness,' added Dillon.

'Yes,' agreed Dad quietly. 'Yes, indeed.'

'Is there more?' asked Dillon, anticipation plain on his face. 'What do I do in the future?'

'Oh, you have lots of adventures, of course,' said Dad, getting back into story-telling mode.

'Tell me, tell me,' pleaded Dillon.

'Well, it seemed that Dillon wasn't the only time traveller,' continued Dad. 'He was followed into the future by the super villain Bilirubin, who had sinister plans to take over the galaxy. It was up to Dillon and his almighty light box to save the day . . .'

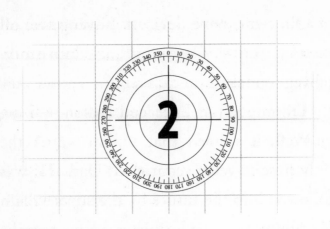

2

Four years later . . .

Dillon squinted into the light. Other-worldly light!

He remembered the tales Dad would tell him when he was younger. But he was eleven now. He could make up his own stories.

Sometimes he imagined he was journeying to a distant planet. Or that the light was part of a time-travelling device, whisking him off into the future. Or that it would give him powers – make him different in a good way. In his mind, the light could do anything he wanted.

But reality was very different. In real life, he needed the light to make him ordinary. To stop his skin from being too yellow. To help his body get rid of the toxic bilirubin.

Bilirubin. It really did sound like a super villain from a sci-fi movie.

Although Dillon would still make up stories about his unusual situation, they no longer had the calming effect they used to. But at least they were a distraction.

He shook his head to clear his thoughts and looked at the book in his hands. Try as he might, he just couldn't concentrate on it today. He closed his copy of *The Time Machine* and put it on the surrounding ledge.

He sighed as he glanced around. The timer was counting down the hours, minutes and seconds. He still had forty-five minutes to go.

Dillon was sitting in a light box, wearing nothing but underwear. His one metre square space was enclosed by four walls, reaching to the height of one and a quarter metres – just up to his head when seated on his little plastic stool. Each wall was made of four Perspex boxes, and each box contained two long ultraviolet lamps. The whole setup had been constructed especially for him by a medical technician from the Women's and Children's Hospital in Adelaide. It was a bit bright, but Dillon was used to it. After all, he'd been under the light for a portion of every day for eleven years, four months and thirteen days.

'Under the light.' That's how Dad referred to it. Dillon preferred to think of it as being *in the light*.

The walls were a bit like shelving units, with a flat surface that created a ledge. There was enough room to put stuff there. Stuff to keep him busy while he sat in the light box for four to six hours every day. Across the ledge today were a short stack of books, two sets of Lego, a model of a Royal Flying Doctor Service aeroplane, some DVDs, a laptop computer and, as always, the digital timer, its glowing green numerals counting down the minutes.

Dillon had a love/hate relationship with the timer. He despised it for the endless moments spent in the light box. But he loved it when the numbers got below an hour. He would sneak glances at the timer from the corner of his eye. He would groan and growl at it when it seemed to be moving too slowly. He would smile at it, when it showed less than what he expected. He had even been known to punch the air with a triumphant 'YES!' when it got to zero.

He glared at it now, willing it to go faster. Then he looked away, his eyes drawn to the model aeroplane. He picked it up and turned it over in his hands. If he were younger he might have flown it through the air around his head, making engine noises. Instead, the flight took place in his mind. He gave the plastic propeller a spin then put the model down again.

What am I going to do now? Dillon sighed. *Maybe I could watch a DVD?*

His eyes scanned the movies Dad had placed there for him. Mostly cartoons. Dillon sighed again, bigger and louder and huffier.

I'm not a little kid anymore, he thought. *I'm almost twelve.*

His eyes came to rest on *Star Wars Episode III*. He groaned.

Why just put one of the Star Wars films? And why number three? Dad knows I like to watch them in order.

He slotted the DVD into the laptop anyway. He had seen the movies often enough that he could even quote the dialogue in many of the scenes.

As the film played, his mind wandered again. This time . . . to the reality of his situation.

The cold, hard facts filled his brain. He had spoken to so many doctors over the years. He had spent hours on the Internet researching his condition. And from a very young age, he had done a lot of eavesdropping.

Adults have this thing about sugar-coating the truth for kids. They find ways of making bad things seem not as bad. But when they are alone, or they think that kids aren't listening . . . well, that's when the truth comes out. Complicated and devastating.

Once at a specialist appointment – after he had been examined, after he had answered the cheery doctor's questions, after he had been given a lollipop and told to go out into the waiting room to play – the door wasn't completely closed. Everyone thought he couldn't hear.

That was the first time he heard the words Crigler-Najjar Syndrome.

Even back then, when he didn't know what it meant, it had sounded scary.

But that's what he had – Crigler-Najjar Syndrome, or CNS for short.

Dillon had been born with this rare genetic disorder. So rare, that less than one in a million people had it. The syndrome affected his liver. It was unable to process and get rid of a toxin called bilirubin. Bilirubin was in everyone's bodies. It was a by-product created by the breakdown of old red blood cells. But unlike Dillon, normal people had livers that worked properly and removed the toxin from the body. The bilirubin would build up inside Dillon, making him sick – and if it wasn't removed, it would kill him.

That's why he had to sit in a light box. It wasn't ordinary light, it was ultraviolet. This type of light was able to get rid of the bilirubin by dissolving it. The problem was, more of it kept building up.

The other thing about CNS was that it made you look weird.

Dillon didn't have any white in his eyes. His black pupils and blue irises floated in a wishy-washy egg-yellow sea. His skin was also yellow-tinged. People were always staring at him or asking him questions.

Why are you so yellow?

What's wrong with your eyes?

Are you sick?

Are you some sort of freak?

People didn't realise how much their comments could hurt.

Back in his light box, Dillon could feel himself getting anxious. His heart was beating a little faster than normal. His palms were slightly tacky. And his mouth was dry.

He hated being different. He wished more than anything that he could be like everyone else.

But wishing didn't work. He knew that way too well.

Dillon remembered wishing with all his might . . .

Two years ago, when Dillon was nine, he had come very close to disaster.

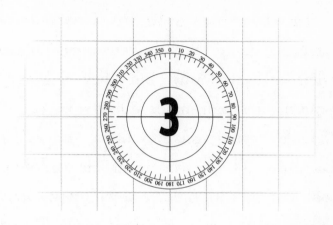

'You look like custard,' one boy teased. 'Custard Face!'

'Or mustard,' said the other boy with a snigger.

'Mustard custard!' said the first boy.

The two looked at each other, then shouted in unison, 'Mustard custard!' They fell about laughing.

School was over for the day. He shouldn't have to put up with this anymore. Dillon tried to walk away, but they followed, pointing and taunting. He sped up.

Dillon could feel eyes upon him as he raced through the schoolyard. He was often looked upon with ridicule or with pity. Both were equally bad. Some kids made fun of him. Others felt sorry for him. Some didn't care. But everyone knew that he was different.

Dillon felt the sting of tears in his own eyes. He sprinted out of the grounds and down the street.

He ran and ran. He didn't really think about where he was going. But it wasn't home. He just wanted to escape – to exhaust his frustration and get it out of his system. His feet pounded on the footpath, his breath heaved in and out and his mind whirled with a confusion of emotions.

He had become pretty good at ignoring what people said about him – to him. But it still hurt, even when he didn't show it. It was hard to conceal what he felt; sometimes he couldn't help reacting. Things had been building up for a few weeks, ever since those two new boys had shown up.

And now he let it all out. Dillon shouted as he ran – a loud, mournful wail.

An elderly man, pruning his roses, glared at Dillon. A lady pushing a pram on the other side of the street stared as he ran past.

Dillon ran off the footpath and across the expanse of green before collapsing under a tree. He leaned against the trunk, gasping for air, and cried.

He wasn't sure how long he was there for, but his eyes were sore and his throat raspy by the time the tears dried up. He pulled a crusty old tissue out of his pocket and wiped his nose.

Finally looking around, Dillon discovered that he was in a park. The leafy trees and the grass beneath made him feel calmer.

I wish I was like everyone else, he thought.

Dillon liked stories. He enjoyed books and films with fantastical plots and impossible things. But he was pretty good at keeping grounded. He knew the difference between fantasy and reality. He knew what his situation was and he knew his disorder wouldn't just go away.

But, right now, he closed his eyes and wished anyway. It was a desperate, heartfelt, aching wish, whispered on a breath.

I wish to be normal.

Of course, it did not come true.

He opened his amber eyes and stared at his jaundiced skin, contrasted against the dark blue of his school uniform. He was very yellow.

Dillon's heart skipped a beat.

He was *too* yellow.

When he was younger, his parents had used a handheld device called a bilirubinometer to measure the amount of toxin in his system. Based on the readings, they knew how much time he had to spend under the lights. But, over the years, they had become pretty good at judging things by the colour of his skin. Looking at his skin now, Dillon knew that he needed more light.

He stared up at the dark, brooding sky. It had been overcast since morning. Without any sun during the day, he would normally go under the lights as soon as he came home after school.

Dillon realised he had no idea what time it was. How long had he been out here? How much time under the lights had he already missed? With storm clouds covering the sky, there was no sun to give him a hint as to how long he'd been in the park. He looked around and realised he didn't even know where he was. He rarely went out on his own. The five-minute walk between home and school was usually it.

I better find my way home, he thought.

He jumped to his feet. His head felt light and he stumbled, sitting down again, hard.

He felt tired and a little unwell. He had not had enough UV light today and the excess bilirubin was beginning to have an effect on him.

He got up slowly and glanced around. He had to get home. Fast! But which way?

A drop of rain hit him on the nose.

Dillon looked up.

Larger drops splattered onto his face and thunder rumbled in the distance. As Dillon headed for the houses beyond the trees, the rain fell in earnest. It was a downpour. It only took seconds for him to be soaked to the skin.

Stumbling from the greenery onto the street, Dillon squinted. He didn't recognise the name on the street sign. The houses were unfamiliar.

Dillon's heart raced as panic set in.

What if I can't find my way home? What if I don't get to the light? I'll get sick. I could die.

Dillon sobbed, unable to decide which way to go. A wave of dizziness washed over him and he realised how tired he was. His legs felt weak and his arms hung limp at his sides.

Is this how it starts? he wondered.

He had never missed a session under the lights before. He wasn't sure what would happen. But he knew it was bad.

Dillon remained standing in the middle of the road, rooted to the spot, shivering.

What am I going to do?

Lights approached, cutting through the dank remains of the day. They were blurry and indistinct, but they moved towards him.

Headlights!

A car pulled up.

There were voices.

And then there were arms around him. Hugging him. Lifting him and bringing him into the car.

It took Dillon a few moments to realise that his parents had located him. Somehow they had found him.

And then he was clinging on to them, as if he might lose them if his grip were too weak.

'I'm sorry,' he sobbed.

The memory still gave Dillon chills.

His parents had rushed him home, dried him off and put him in the light box.

The next day there was a visit to the doctor and a hearing check. Excess bilirubin could collect around the brainstem. The first effect would be on hearing. So regular six-monthly hearing checks were a part of Dillon's life. After finding him at the park, so much more yellow than usual, an extra hearing check seemed like a good idea. Thankfully, everything had been okay.

Dillon swallowed. Hard. He shifted uncomfortably on the plastic stool in his light box.

What would have happened if his hearing had been affected? If the build-up of bilirubin had continued? Deafness would have been the next stage. And then his intellectual development would have been affected. And then . . .

Dillon took a deep breath and shuddered. He didn't want to think about it.

Dillon knew he wasn't like everyone else. He knew there was no point in wishing to be normal.

He tried to focus instead on what made him feel good – his home.

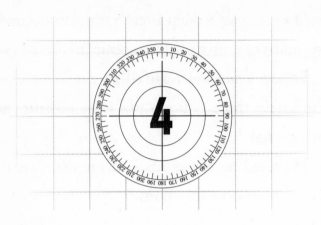

Dillon lived in a street called Faith, which was in a suburb called Hope Valley. The suburb belonged to the City of Adelaide, in the state of South Australia, in the country of Australia, which was in the Asia–Pacific region of the planet Earth. That planet was in a relatively small solar system within the Milky Way galaxy, which was but a small part of the greater Universe. Of course, beyond that was the theoretical multiverse with all its parallel realities.

That's how Dillon liked to think of where he lived. It made him feel part of something infinitely larger than him. It allowed him to imagine that maybe his situation, his problems, his genetic disorder, were actually not as big and all-consuming as they often felt.

His location made him feel alive.

Hope Valley was a leafy area with trees and parks, and although the grass often browned and dried in the hot summer months, it would always return. And Dillon was only a few streets away from a reservoir. If you looked it up on Google Earth, which he often did, you would see the splash of blue encased in greenery. Blue and green. Water and vegetation. The colours of life.

Dillon had done a lot of exploring, both online and in real life, after his running away incident. He'd decided he needed to know the area in which he lived like the back of his hand so that he'd never get lost again. He liked that phrase, 'like the back of his hand'. It often appeared in stories, and this was something from a story that he could apply to real life.

He liked his street name, Faith. And he appreciated the name of his suburb, Hope Valley. Faith and Hope. It seemed to sum up how he felt about things. Despite his fears, Dillon was hopeful about the future – that things would get better for him and that he'd be able to live a normal life.

And in order to have hope in the future, he needed to have faith in the doctors. He needed to believe that they would come through. That they would get him what he needed . . .

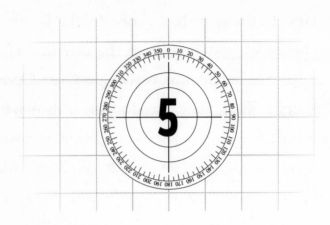

Dillon shielded his eyes from the light. It didn't usually bother him, but right now he wished he was wearing a pair of sunglasses. He closed his eyes instead, shifting uncomfortably on his plastic stool.

Eventually the light would not be enough. Eventually the bilirubin would build up to toxic levels. Eventually he would die.

Unless . . .

He got what he needed . . .

And what he needed was a new liver. One that worked.

But getting a new liver scared him almost as much as not getting one. Although he had faith and hope, fear and doubt often fought with them. It was a constant battle.

The idea of doctors cutting him open, ripping out one of his organs and stuffing in a new one filled him with dread. He had talked to his best friend, Jay, about it . . .

Jayden, or Jay as he preferred, was bigger than Dillon. While Dillon was slim and fair,

Jay was broad and dark. A recent growth spurt also put him a head taller.

'Operations aren't that scary,' Jay insisted. 'Lots of people have 'em. I've had one and I'm okay.'

'You had appendicitis,' said Dillon. 'That's a bit ordinary. This is a transplant. It's terrifying!'

'Dude,' said Jay. 'My appendix exploded! There was pus floating around in my insides. They yanked what was left of my burst appendix out of me. Then they had to vacuum up all that gloop. I could've died, you know!'

'Yeah, all right,' conceded Dillon. 'It sounds pretty gross.' He hesitated. 'But still. Mine's a transplant.'

'Dude!' There was that word again. Jay liked it way too much and said it in a poor imitation of a surfer. 'You've gotta chill! Either you get the transplant, or you spend your life getting a tan.'

Dillon laughed. Jay always called the light box a tanning salon. But then his expression became grave. 'It's more than that,' he said, voice quavering slightly. 'If I don't get a new liver, things will get worse.'

'Worse?' asked Jay. 'How?'

'The UV light doesn't work as well when you get older,' explained Dillon. 'At some point it'll stop working and I'll . . .' He swallowed. 'I'll get sick . . . and . . . and then I'll die.'

'How long?' asked Jay, his voice now a serious whisper.

'Not sure,' said Dillon. 'I heard my mum and dad talking about it a couple of months ago. They reckon that problems start after puberty. Something about my skin getting tougher and the light not being as effective.'

'Dude!' Jay let that word hang there for a while. 'Dude.' He shook his head. 'If it's life or death, you gotta go the transplant.'

'Yeah,' agreed Dillon. 'I know. But it's a scary thought.'

It was scary indeed. And it had become even more scary since.

Six weeks ago, Dillon had gone to the Royal Children's Hospital in Melbourne for a transplant operation. Everything had been set to go – he was in a room, dressed in a hospital gown, his mum waiting nervously with him. And then came the blood test to check for the suitability of the transplant. Unfortunately the donor liver had not been compatible and Dillon returned to Adelaide with his old, faulty organ still inside of him.

It had been devastating. His parents spent days in a gloom, barely speaking to each other. It was as if not talking about it meant that it hadn't happened. And it was better to wipe the whole incident rather than have to admit it might happen again.

The possibility had never occurred to Dillon before then. He'd always believed that when a liver was available, it would just be a matter of putting it in. But apparently it wasn't. It had to be compatible. And even then, there was a chance of his body rejecting it.

What would happen then? he reflected. *If my old liver is gone and my body won't accept the new one . . . can I live without a liver? Or will I die?*

A space battle on the computer screen brought him out of his thoughts and back into the reality of his light box. He realised that his hands were sweating. He felt a quivering in his stomach and a pounding in his chest. He took a deep breath and tried to calm himself down.

He tried to think of all the good things in his life.

He had fair skin. It might seem like an odd thing to be happy about, but Dillon's paleness allowed the UV light to work more effectively. It meant less time in the light. And his blond hair meant that the yellowness of his skin wasn't as noticeable as it might otherwise be. It would be far more obvious if contrasted to dark hair.

Dillon started to feel a little better.

Good things, he told himself. *Concentrate on good things.*

He had a best friend. He had parents who he loved dearly.

And cricket! He enjoyed playing cricket. And today had been a good day for it. He tried to fill his mind with the events of the day . . .

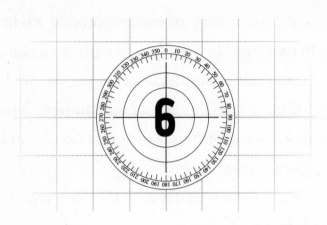

Things got off to an early start. The alarm blared at 6.30 am.

Dillon usually hit the snooze button on school mornings, trying to squeeze in a few extra minutes in bed. But today was Saturday and he wasn't going to school. He jumped straight out of bed and slid into the cricket whites draped over the back of a chair.

Mum had breakfast on the table as he bounded into the kitchen.

'You're chipper this morning,' she said, brushing a strand of mousy brown hair from her eyes. She was of average height and a little on the plump side. Wide, friendly eyes shone from her round face, projecting a feeling of warmth.

Dillon grinned. 'Got a good feeling about the match.'

He sat down and devoured the bacon and pancakes, which he first drowned in maple syrup. This was a get-your-own-breakfast household most mornings, which usually meant cereal for Dillon. But Mum always made something special on a match day.

Dillon was out the door by seven, in the car and being driven to Jay's place by Dad.

Dad was tall and gangly, but with a small round belly that looked out of place. His thinning hair was a greying blond and he had pasty white skin with loads of freckles. He yawned every couple of minutes as they drove. He didn't like mornings.

They arrived at Jay's just before 7.15 am.

Dad honked the horn. Dillon pulled at his seatbelt impatiently.

A couple of minutes later, Jay stumbled out of the house.

'Good luck, Jayden,' his mum's voice called from inside.

Jay threw his sports bag into the boot, then fell into the back seat of the car. 'Yo!' he grunted.

'Yo right back at you,' said Dad with a smirk.

Jay clicked the belt into place, leaned his face against the window and closed his eyes.

'Come on,' said Dillon, looking at his friend. 'You can't be tired. You've got to be on your best game.'

'I'll be fine when the time comes,' said Jay sleepily, without opening his eyes.

Dillon poked him in the ribs. Jay grunted.

Dillon stared out the window for the next half hour. The sky was clear and blue. It looked set to be a bright sunny day. Which is exactly what Dillon liked. It would mean less time in his light box. The sun's warming glow included ultraviolet light. And he would be out in it all morning.

The car pulled into the parking lot of the sportsground at 7.46 am. A number of cars were already there, and a bus was pulling in behind them.

'We're here,' said Dillon, stabbing a finger into Jay's ribs again before getting out.

Jay's eyes snapped open and he sprung from the car, suddenly awake and enthused. 'Ta-da!' He flung out his arms. 'Told you I'd be ready.'

Dillon laughed. 'And people say I'm weird.'

'Good luck,' said Dad through the open window. 'See you after the match.'

The two boys grabbed their bags and headed for the pavilion. An umpire was out on the oval, examining the pitch. A few people were hanging around the edges of the grass.

At eight on the dot, the coach gave them their pep talk. He was large, overweight and bald. He looked fierce, but spoke with a gentle lilt to his voice. He spoke about strategy, playing to your strengths and having fun.

The coin was tossed at 8.14 am. Dillon punched the air – their side would bat first. Batting was his strength.

He was up third.

The first two batters were doing well until a yorker from the opposition, coming in at the crease, took out the stumps.

It was Dillon's turn now.

Butterflies were flying loop-the-loops in his stomach as he walked to the pitch. He had been a star batsman in junior cricket last year. His first season in his school's senior team had been okay, but not brilliant. But he was feeling optimistic about today.

Dillon reached the crease, positioned himself and felt the butterflies scatter. He was never nervous while batting. His anxiety would rise as he waited for his turn and would go with him to the pitch, but as he took a deep breath in preparation to bat, it would disappear.

Dillon watched the ball as the bowler tossed it into the air and caught it. He did not take his eyes from it. He paid no attention to the bowler, couldn't even tell you what he looked like. All his attention was focused on that red sphere as it was carried in the run up and released, hurtling down the pitch towards him.

He pulled the bat back and swung, the jarring sensation travelling up his arms and through his body like a wave as the ball connected with the bat.

The ball soared into the air and he ran. It landed on the grass, to be quickly scooped up by a fielder and thrown back.

Two runs.

He hit his next ball low.

One run.

His third ball came in super fast, right at the crease. He took a step forward and smashed it on the full with all his might.

He heard the cheering halfway down the pitch.

'SIX!' called the umpire.

Another cheer went up from the spectators.

His first six for the season! His first six in senior cricket!

Dillon scored another twenty runs before being caught out. A total of twenty-nine. He was happy with that.

The rest of the match streaked past in a blur of motion. Runs were scored, balls were caught, stumps were smashed. The game was close, but they won. And Dillon's six was the only one of the match.

Dad took him and Jay out for milkshakes to celebrate. They sat at the café's outside table. The three of them clinked their glasses together in a victory toast and Jay said, 'You're the dude!'

As Dillon slurped the last of his shake, he looked up and enjoyed the feel of the sun's warmth on his face. His skin felt tingly and he imagined the ultraviolet light doing its work ... like a cricket bat smashing the bilirubin out of his system – hitting it for a six!

He returned home on a wave of excitement, barely able to stop talking.

Even his mum's complaints about the state of his room couldn't diminish the thrill of having scored a six. He promised to clean his room tomorrow.

Dinner was spaghetti bolognaise. His favourite.

And then it was into the light box.

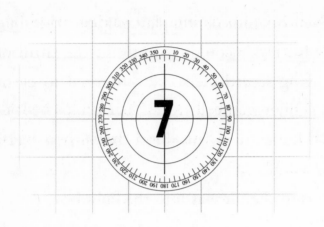

Dillon finally got out of the box at 11.30 pm. It had been a long day and he was tired.

He went straight to bed, but found himself staring at the ceiling, his mind replaying the six. It was a good reason to have difficulty in falling asleep.

Finally, be began to doze off . . . only to

be dragged back into the waking world by a loud ringing.

The phone!

Dillon glanced at the clock on his bedside table. Who in the world would be ringing at 12.30 am?

And then his heart skipped a beat. *Could it be?*

He tried to calm down. *It could be anything*, he told himself. *A wrong number. A telemarketer working late. The death of a long-lost family member.*

Or . . .

It might be a new liver.

Unconsciously, he found himself crossing his fingers and holding his breath as he listened.

The ring cut off as the phone was answered.

'Hello?' Mum's weary voice carried through the silent house.

There were a few seconds of silence. Then . . .

'What?' Her voice was excited.

There was movement. Mum was walking around the house as she spoke, her words now muffled and indistinct.

Dillon got out of bed and crept to his door. He opened it and listened.

'Yes!' Mum was almost shouting now. 'Yes, yes. Thank you. Thank you so much.'

Dillon's heart was pounding hard and his breath was coming in short rasping bursts. His mind was whirling with the possibilities and hope.

Mum hung up the phone and came racing down the corridor. She ran straight to Dillon and wrapped her arms around him, almost lifting him off the floor.

'They've got a liver!' she whispered.

Dillon's knees turned to jelly. If Mum hadn't been holding on to him, he was sure he would have fallen over. And it seemed to be forever before she finally let go.

Dillon leaned up against the wall to steady himself. Dad appeared at the other end of the corridor, bleary-eyed and tousle-haired.

'What's up?' he asked, confused with sleep.

'They've got a liver!' Mum shouted as she ran to embrace him.

Dad's eyes were now awake and alert. Dillon smiled as his parents hugged and did a little happy dance. Then Mum stopped and looked back at Dillon.

'They're getting a Flying Doctors aeroplane ready. We need to get moving,' she called. 'NOW!'

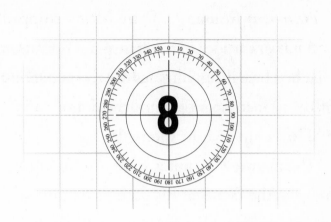

Dillon was shaking as he stuffed his iPod and iPad into his overnight bag. It was already full of clothes, waiting for the time it would be needed.

Could this really be it? he thought.

He suddenly realised that he may have had his last session in the light box. If all went well, he would never have to sit in it again.

Is this my future?

And yet the idea of the transplant operation weighed heavily on him. As did the possibility of being incompatible with the donor.

'Hurry up!' Mum shouted.

The next few minutes were utterly frantic. Despite the fact that his parents had insisted on preparing a plan in advance (including a list, maps, where to park at the airport, etc.), they still seemed to be running around like headless chooks.

Finally, they headed out the door. In theory, Dillon was never supposed to be more than half an hour from an airport, in case the call came. But Hope Valley was about forty minutes' drive away in daytime traffic. In the middle of the night, however, half an hour should be easy.

Dillon sat in the back of the car, while his parents got into the front.

Dad paused for a moment, holding the key in the ignition. Dillon heard him take a long, deep breath. He let it out slowly.

'Ready?' Dad asked so quietly it was almost a whisper.

'I think so.' Mum's voice was a little timid and shaky.

'You bet!' answered Dillon with enthusiasm.

His parents nodded in unison and Dad turned the key.

Dillon smiled as the engine started.

Best day ever, thought Dillon.

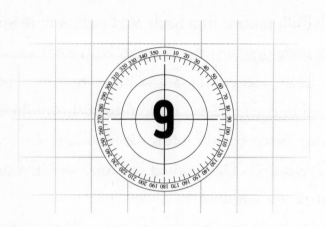

Dillon watched the street lights go by, glowing points in the darkness. His eyes went from one to the next, like a gigantic dot-to-dot illuminating the night.

He imagined the patterns and pictures they might form when viewed from above. Instantly, it transported him six weeks back in time, to his first flight aboard an

RFDS plane. There was no faster way to get to Melbourne for a transplant, than with the Royal Flying Doctor Service.

Like this time, the call had come in the evening, although not as late. *Do all transplants happen then?* he wondered. Dillon had been whisked away into the car by his parents, taken to the airport and flown to Melbourne. He had always assumed that the Flying Doctors only ever dealt with emergencies in far-off, out-of-the-way places. But it seemed that they also did short-notice, middle-of-the-night transfers in city locations.

He remembered looking out of the window as the plane rose higher – watching the lights grow more distant. They did make patterns. The higher the plane went, the more intricate the patterns became. And he could see pictures in the lights — faces, animals, machinery. His imagination ran wild until the landscape changed, leaving behind the illumination.

His mind returned to the present with a sudden lurch.

The car was pulling over, making an odd thumping sound.

'What's wrong?' asked Dillon.

'Just a flat tyre,' said Dad with an exasperated sigh. 'Talk about rotten timing.'

'What are we going to do?' demanded Mum, voice rising.

'Change the tyre,' said Dad, deadpan, opening his door.

The three of them got out of the car and stood back. The tyre on the front passenger side was indeed flat. On closer examination, Dad found a nail embedded in the rubber.

'We're going to be late,' worried Mum, running her hands through her hair.

Dillon's heart jumped. *Late? We can't be late!* Every step of the way, it had been drummed into them how essential speed was in the case of an organ transplant.

'It's going to be okay,' said Dad. 'I'm good with tyres. I'll have it replaced within ten minutes.'

'That's still ten minutes late,' said Mum, pacing anxiously on the footpath. 'You know how important it is to get Dillon to the hospital immediately.' She stopped, an idea springing into mind. 'Maybe Dillon and I should take a taxi?'

Dad was already getting the spare and the jack out of the boot. 'In the time it takes you to ring and wait for a taxi, we'll be ready to go. But go ahead, if you like.' He winked at Dillon. 'We can make it a race. See if I can get us going before the taxi arrives.'

Dillon laughed. Mum's attention snapped to him, her face tense. But then she relaxed and nodded. 'Okay. How about I ring and let the RFDS know what's happened?'

'Excellent idea,' said Dad as he started jacking up the car.

Mum walked off behind them. Making that call would keep her busy and out of Dad's way. It would also help her stay calm.

'Need a hand?' asked Dillon, eager to participate.

'No, no,' assured Dad, getting to work on loosening the wheel nuts. 'I've got this.'

Dillon sighed. Whenever Dad refused assistance, it made Dillon wonder: *Is it because I'm defective?*

Was Dad trying to protect him? Or didn't he think he was capable? Or was it just coincidence?

Whatever the case, it made Dillon feel left out. Excluded from the details of his own adventure.

With nothing else to do, Dillon worried. He worried about getting the transplant, about not getting the transplant, about the possibility of another incompatible liver. But mostly, he worried about being late.

What if this delay stuffs up everything?

Being quick was important when it came to transplanting organs. A liver would only be viable for transplant for a certain amount of time after the donor had died . . . although he wasn't really sure how long that was. No one had actually told him that. But he thought that it was different from case to case, depending on the circumstances of death. Either way, he didn't want to miss his opportunity because of a stupid flat tyre.

Mum finished her call and walked back to the car to see that it was fixed.

'And that would be a new family record,' said Dad, heaving the replaced wheel into the boot and tossing the jack in after it.

'Fastest tyre-changer in the West,' quipped Mum. Now that everything was okay again, she seemed more ready to joke about it.

'Maybe we should apply to the *Guinness World Records*?' suggested Dad.

'Or maybe we should just get going?' said Mum. 'Come on.'

They all got back into the car. Dad paused like he had earlier, holding the key in the ignition.

'Ready?' he asked, after taking a long, deep breath.

'Oh, would you just get moving!' demanded Mum.

'Right-oh, then.' Dad turned the key and the engine started. 'Fingers crossed for smooth sailing from here on in.'

Sailing? thought Dillon. *We're in a car, not a boat.* He often considered Dad's choice of analogy to be a bit weird.

The car took off, zooming up the deserted road.

'Well, that was a bit of an adventure,' said Dad.

'Let's hope there aren't any more,' countered Mum.

A flat tyre is nothing, thought Dillon. *The transplant is going to be the real adventure.*

The rest of the journey to the airport was uneventful. They arrived at 1.25 am, parked and made their way to the RFDS Aeromedical Base in the north-west of the airport. It was positioned along with the charter services, between the main terminal and the car rental places.

A woman in dark blue trousers and a

light blue short-sleeved shirt approached them as they arrived. The logo on her shirt immediately identified her as an RFDS nurse. She was tying her long blonde hair into a high ponytail as she walked.

'Hello,' she said cheerily, readjusting her red-rimmed glasses. 'You must be the Grayson family.'

'That'd be us,' answered Dad, stifling a yawn. 'Excuse me.'

'No worries,' said the nurse, eyes bright and alive. 'It's rather late to be out and about.'

'You seem to be handling it better than us,' said Dad, heading into small-talk mode. He did it automatically whenever he was anxious – as if talking about normal, ordinary things would make everything okay.

'Been doing shift work for many years now,' said the nurse. 'You get used to it pretty quick. And I rather like night flights.' She turned her attention to Dillon. 'Dillon, I presume. My name's Felicity and I'm very pleased to make your acquaintance.' She stuck out her hand.

Dillon shook it awkwardly. 'Ah . . . hi.'

'There's no need to be nervous,' Felicity went on. 'This is all pretty standard. Follow me.' With a flick of her ponytail she turned and strode off. 'By the way,' she called over her shoulder, 'you can call me Flick'.

Mum and Dad shrugged in unison and followed, Dillon bringing up the rear.

Flick led them into the almost empty terminal, through a door that bypassed the metal detectors and X-ray machines, and onto the tarmac.

'There she is,' announced Flick, pointing to the RFDS plane.

'A Pilatus PC-12,' piped up Dillon, his eyes going over the plane in the airport lights.

The plane looked very sporty, with its white body, red undercarriage and blue tail. Even though it only had one propeller, it still said 'speed' to Dillon.

Flick turned to him, a little surprised. 'Well informed, aren't you?'

'I've been on one,' said Dillon. 'About six weeks ago.'

'He liked it so much,' said Dad, 'that we got him a toy model.'

'So you've flown with us before?' said Flick. 'Why was that?'

'It was a false alarm,' explained Mum. 'We went to Melbourne for a donor liver, but after doing tests they realised it wasn't a match.'

'Oh, I'm sorry to hear that,' said Flick. 'Hopefully things will be better this time.' She turned to Mum and Dad. 'Now, which of you will be accompanying our patient today? As you know, there's only room for one extra passenger.'

'I'm coming,' said Mum.

'And I'll join them later in the day,' added Dad. 'Assuming all's clear for the transplant.'

'We're good to go straight away,' said Flick. 'So I shall say goodbye to you, Mr Grayson.'

She lifted a hand and waved, smiling all the while. 'Goodbye. And the rest of us may now board.' She headed towards the plane.

'Good luck, son,' said Dad, giving Dillon a tight, bone-crushing hug. 'I'll be thinking of you.'

After he had also hugged Mum, she and Dillon followed Flick up the stairs and into the cabin. It was all very familiar. As before, Dillon marvelled at this flying hospital room.

Two stretchers were attached to one wall; monitors, IV drips and other equipment secured around them.

Dillon and Mum took the two seats that faced each other. Flick closed the door, the stairs hinging up to seal off the cabin.

'All set, Igor,' she called, sitting in the seat closest to the cockpit.

'Igor?' asked Dillon with a smirk, thinking back to the old black-and-white horror films he had watched with Dad. They were more funny than scary. 'Does that mean Frankenstein's on board as well?'

'No, it does not,' responded a low, gruff voice with just the hint of an accent.

Dillon and Mum stared towards the cockpit as a short man with a bushy dark moustache and sideburns appeared in the doorway. He wore a blue flight jacket zipped up right to the neck. He was chewing on something. Glaring from person to person, he swallowed, then sucked air through his teeth.

'I am the pilot,' said Igor, 'not a mad scientist's henchman.'

Dillon felt his face redden. 'I . . . I'm sorry.'

'Not to worry,' said Igor, his face breaking into an unexpected grin. Dillon noticed he had food stuck in his teeth. 'It is a common mistake. I am called Igor Vyacheslavovich Maspnov.'

'He's Russian,' said Flick, by way of explanation.

'No, no,' corrected Igor. 'My parents are Russian. Me, I am a true-blue, dinky-di Aussie.' And as if to prove it, he added a 'G'day, mate!' before disappearing back into the cockpit.

Dillon and Mum looked at each other. This pilot was very different to the one on their last flight. That other pilot had seemed like he had walked out of a flight-school brochure – tall, blond, neat and very official, using words like 'wilco', 'affirmative' and 'roger'. Igor was something else.

Flick shrugged. 'You get used to him.'

'Okay.' Igor's voice now came over the speakers. 'Strap yourselves in. We are good to go.'

Dillon hurriedly secured his seatbelt for safety.

The cabin rattled as the engine roared into life. With a little jerk the plane began to taxi along the runway, the whine of machinery increasing.

'Here we go again,' said Mum, hopefully.

Dillon nodded then pressed his face up against the window. He took a deep breath and looked out at the airport, splashes of light illuminating the buildings and planes. The hum and shake of his surroundings faded into the distance as he gazed into the beckoning night. He barely even noticed the aircraft lifting off.

The events of the day fell away.

His worries about the future melted like snowflakes in the sun.

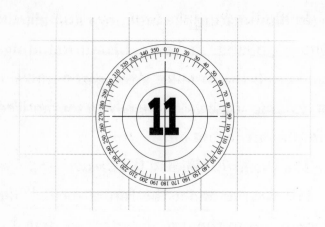

11

As the plane flew over populated areas, Dillon played his game of dot-to-dot. When the lights were all gone and they were flying over unseen desert landscape, he returned his attention to the cabin.

He noticed Mum looking at him with a strange expression – a mixture of hope and fear.

Immediately, his own anxieties came flooding back.

Will this be another false alarm? Will a blood test send me straight home, like last time? Or will I get a new liver?

But the possibility of the operation going ahead was just as frightening as it not going ahead. Visions of a scalpel cutting into his flesh, blood spurting everywhere, burned in his mind. Hands reaching inside of him and pulling out a red, meaty organ . . .

'I'm a nurse,' announced Flick, the words dispelling the images from Dillon's mind. 'So if there's anything you'd like to know about your upcoming procedure, feel free to ask.' She spoke loudly, precisely, like an actor projecting on stage, in order to be heard over the sound of the engine.

'Um,' Dillon looked at Mum. 'I think we pretty much know everything already.'

The last thing Dillon wanted to do was talk about the operation. That would just make him more nervous.

'Yes,' agreed Mum. 'We've been on the organ donor waiting list for about two years. We've had a lot of time to study up and prepare.'

'Too much time,' added Dillon.

'Okay,' said Flick. 'Just remember that I'm here should you change your mind and want to ask anything.' She settled back in her seat.

'I guess this must be kinda boring for you,' said Dillon, trying to make conversation. 'Kind of like babysitting.'

'If you think babysitting is boring, it probably means that you've never tried it!'

said Flick with a little laugh. 'Babysitting my nephews is like trying to arrange a meditation session in the middle of a war zone. Anyway, in this line of work, boring is good. The non-boring flights are usually emergency situations.'

'Do you get many boring flights?' asked Mum, joining in.

'Actually, yes.' Flick leaned forward, obviously happy to talk. 'Well, I don't like to think of them as boring. Even if my nursing skills aren't required on a flight, I still get to meet interesting people.' She smiled at Dillon as she said this. 'The RFDS do quite a lot of transfer flights. People being taken from one hospital to another. I suppose most of those could be described as routine rather than boring. The patient is often in a stable condition and we're just getting them to a specialist. But we'd still have to do obs.'

Dillon looked quizzically at her.

'Sorry. "Obs" is short for observations. It's nurse talk. It means checking things like blood pressure, heart rate, temperature. But in your case, I don't need to really do anything. It's more of an aerial taxi service because we're the only plane free at this time of night at such short notice.'

'We're very thankful that you are available,' said Mum, rather more earnestly than needed.

Dillon pondered what would have happened to him if there was no RFDS. It didn't bear thinking about.

'Just doing our jobs,' Flick assured them with a warm smile.

Dillon yawned.

'Perhaps you should get some sleep,' suggested Flick. 'You look pretty tired. And we've still got about an hour and twenty minutes before we get there.'

'I don't think I can,' said Dillon. 'Too nervous.'

'And I'm certainly not going to nap,' added Mum.

'Couldn't hurt to try,' said Flick.

'How old are your nephews?' asked Mum, wanting a conversation to distract her.

'Four and seven,' answered Flick.

Then the two of them were off on an in-depth discussion about how wonderful little kids were and about how they grow up too fast and about all the cute things they did before growing up too fast.

Boring.

Dillon closed his eyes as the voices droned on.

There was a voice in the distance that sounded like it was talking through a loudspeaker.

Dillon opened his eyes.

'Hello there, sleepyhead,' said Flick. 'Good to see you took my advice. We're not far now. Perfect time to wake up – Igor just asked if you wanted to come into the cockpit.'

'Yeah!' Dillon tried to spring from his seat, forgetting his belt. 'Oooooph!' His face heated up with embarrassment as he unbuckled himself and made his way to the end of the cabin.

'Hi,' said Dillon, looking into the cockpit.

'Hi yourself,' answered Igor. 'Have a sit.'

Dillon manoeuvred his way into the seat next to Igor. It was padded and more comfortable than the one he had in the cabin. He gazed at the instrumentation in front of him – a confusing array of switches, dials, knobs, lights, displays. And two steering wheels – one for each seat.

'Um, shouldn't you have a co-pilot?' asked Dillon nervously.

'He was late so I left without him,' answered Igor.

'What?' Panic leaped up into Dillon's throat.

'Kidding!' said Igor. 'Relax, I don't need a co-pilot. It's not part of standard procedures. Having one pilot on standby is expensive enough.' He chuckled to himself and Dillon wasn't sure if he was joking again.

Dillon's eyes returned to the dashboard. There were two screens in the centre that reminded him of the one in the fancy new hybrid car his parents bought a couple of months ago. The first screen displayed a navigational chart and the other a series of complex-looking readings, mostly numbers. Dillon let out a long breath.

'It's not as complicated as it seems,' Igor assured him. 'And once you're up in the air it's mostly automatic, anyway. I'm just here for show.' He chuckled again, deep and hearty.

Dillon looked through the windscreen. In the distance he could see a large cluster of lights. 'Is that Melbourne?' he asked.

'Sure is,' said Igor. 'Beautiful from up here, isn't it?'

'Uh-huh,' agreed Dillon.

'Especially in the dark,' continued Igor. 'I love the lights at night, like little explosions of joy in the lonely blackness. As you get closer the lights multiply. One dot becomes many. And every dot brightens the lives of many people. It is magnificent.'

'Yes,' said Dillon slowly, awestruck by the sight and the concept. 'Yes, it is.'

I could stay up here forever, he thought. *Above everything. Beyond all my problems and fears.*

Igor's arm shot out and his hand zipped over the controls.

'This is Flying-Doctor-5-4-1,' said Igor, adjusting his headset. He listened a moment,

then continued. 'We have a patient transfer for the organ donor program, so, yes, it is important we land ASAP.' He paused a moment and his voice rose. 'Why? What's happening?' He paused again. 'Could you please . . . actually, hold on.' He covered the microphone with his hand and turned to Dillon, any trace of cheer and humour gone from his face. 'I'm going to have to ask you to return to the cabin now, thank you.'

Dillon's heart was racing as he got up. In his hurry he banged his hip into the back of the seat, then rushed out.

Mum took one look at his expression as he returned and immediately leaned forward to ask: 'What's wrong?'

'I don't know,' said Dillon, panic rising. 'Something.'

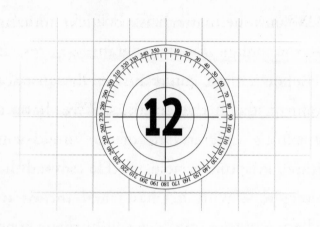

12

Dillon and his mum looked at each other with mounting worry. There had been no word from Igor since Dillon had left the cockpit. Not knowing what was going on was stressful. It might not be anything to be concerned about but, then again, it could be some sort of disaster.

'What's the matter?' asked Flick, noticing their exchange of worried glances.

Before Dillon could answer, Igor's voice boomed from the speakers: 'We have a bit of a situation. One of the runways is temporarily out of commission. Something is wrong with the lights. They are down to using one runway for all arrivals and departures, and there is a backlog of freight planes circling and waiting to land. I've stressed the importance of our situation and am now awaiting further instruction.' Dillon heard a long, deep intake of breath. 'So, for now, we're stuck up here.'

'Delay?' Mum's eyes were wide and concerned. 'What about the transplant? We were told we had to get there as quickly as possible.'

A tremor ran through Dillon's body. First a flat tyre, now an airport delay – nothing was going right.

'Let's not get too concerned yet,' said Flick, her voice calm and even. 'The delay may only be short. And even if it is a while, that doesn't necessarily mean the transplant has to be cancelled. There is usually some leeway in terms of timing.'

'I hope you're right,' said Mum, folding her arms and leaning back in her chair, her face a stony mask.

May only be short? *Doesn't necessarily mean*? *Usually some leeway*? *That doesn't sound all that reassuring*, thought Dillon.

Flick unbuckled her belt and got up. 'I'm going to check in with Igor and also see if

I can get a message to the Royal Children's Hospital.'

As she disappeared into the cockpit, Dillon leaned his head against the window. The cold glass felt good against his forehead. Below, hundreds of lights were twinkling.

What had Igor called them? Little explosions of joy in the lonely blackness.

Right now, they just made Dillon feel alone. He was so far above them, and he couldn't get down. He was separated from the lights – isolated.

He tried to connect the dots, but it just wouldn't work. There were no pictures, no patterns. Just chaos. And in that chaos, he knew, one of those lights was the hospital where a liver waited for him.

Dillon had spent all this time fearing the transplant. But now that it was in jeopardy, he suddenly realised how much he wanted it – how much he craved the life it offered him. He choked back the sob that tried to push its way up.

Flick came bustling back. 'Everything is going to be all right,' she said. 'Igor said that flight control were working on getting us down immediately. And I've spoken to the hospital. There will be an ambulance waiting when we land, which will take you straight there. It will be okay.'

Dillon nodded, but wouldn't allow himself to get his hopes up. He looked back to the window. Still, the lights were just lights.

'Good news, people.' Igor's voice was cheery. 'Buckle up. We're coming in to land.'

'See?' said Flick. 'I told you it would be fine.'

Mum sighed with relief.

Dillon felt wobbly, like a tub of jelly. He must have been holding himself so tense, and now that he relaxed, he felt shaky. He was sure that if he had been standing, he would probably have collapsed.

'I guess this flight wasn't quite as boring as you were expecting,' said Flick.

Dillon nodded and looked back out the window. There, in the lights, he could see a smiling face – welcoming them as they descended.

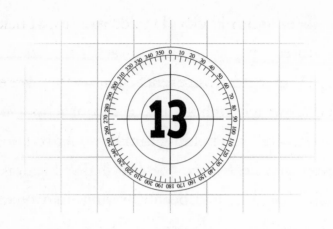

As with the takeoff, Dillon was glued to the window for the landing. The aeroplane touched down at 3.55 am.

'My stomach always flips when a plane lands or takes off,' said Mum, when they were down.

'Does it?' asked Dillon, his attention returning to the cabin. 'It doesn't bother me.'

When the plane had taxied to a stop, Flick released the door and lowered the stairs. Igor emerged from the cockpit as they were about to disembark.

'Apologies for the delay,' he said. 'But we have you here now. Good luck, young man. I hope that all goes well for you today and in the future, and that you see the lights from the night sky many more times.'

'Thank you, sir,' said Dillon.

Flick led Dillon and Mum along the tarmac towards a waiting ambulance. Dillon took one last glance at the aircraft; its white body with streaks of red and blue bathed in the airport lights.

Could I ever fly a plane like that?

'And this is where I say goodbye,' announced Flick as the ambulance driver stepped forward to meet them. 'It's been a pleasure accompanying you on a mostly boring flight.'

Mum laughed and Dillon grinned.

'Who wants to ride up front?' asked the ambulance driver.

Dillon looked immediately at Mum, who nodded. 'Sure. I don't mind sitting in the back,' she said.

The driver didn't say much on the journey, preferring to turn up the radio. Majestic classical music resounded through the vehicle as it sped along the Tullamarine Freeway towards the large cluster of lights that was Melbourne. The strings soared and the trumpets blared, the piano danced and the symbols clashed, all in perfect accompaniment to the passing view.

There weren't many cars on the road just after four in the morning. The ambulance streaked along, passing the few vehicles that were out there. Dillon connected street lamp to street lamp as they went, creating a glowing line from airport to hospital on the map in his mind. He didn't really know the layout of this city, but he imagined the route as a swirly sweeping pattern, meandering and beautiful.

Dillon was disappointed that they drove without the siren. He would have liked the drama of flashing lights and wailing sound. It would have made the drive more of an event. The driver laughed when he asked about the siren and simply said 'we don't need it' without any further explanation.

There were a few more cars when they got off the freeway.

Dillon's heart skipped a beat as they approached the Royal Children's Hospital, the gleaming structure ablaze with light. It was strikingly beautiful – curves and glass and coloured panels. It didn't look like a hospital at all. But it was. A hospital full of children.

They pulled into an ambulance bay and hopped out. It was the middle of the night but things still seemed busy. There were other ambulances parked around them. A little kid on a stretcher was being unloaded from one, and off to the side a small group of nurses chatted intensely.

Their driver took them to the reception desk, where Mum gave their details and filled out forms. It seemed a bit like checking into a hotel. Not that Dillon had ever actually done that – but he'd watched people on television. And then a plastic name tag was secured to his wrist.

It felt like a long time, but he finally found himself in a room changing into a hospital gown. He thought it was really stupid, how it did up at the back. Even when it was tied up, it was as if his gown was gaping and his bum was out on display. He climbed into the bed as quickly as he could and waited some more. Mum sat on the chair by his bed.

Soon, a nurse came to take a blood sample. His blood would be put into a machine and separated to create what was called a serum, which contained his body's antibodies.

Antibodies were what helped your body fight off sickness. But they could also react with other foreign elements . . . such as a transplanted organ. His serum would be mixed with white blood cells from the donor organ. And then the doctors would check to see if the antibodies reacted – if they would fight against the donor organ.

Dillon imagined his antibodies as soldiers, going to war against potential diseases. He hoped that they would recognise this new liver as an ally rather than an enemy. He had a silly cartoon-like vision of tiny troops charging a massive, bloated liver in the middle of a green field. The liver had a face with a frightened expression and it held a white flag in its pudgy little hands.

'Attack!' yelled the captain, and just as the troops were about to strike, a courier on a World War II motorcycle raced up with a message from headquarters: 'Cease fire! Do not attack!'

Dillon chuckled as he hoped that his antibodies would listen to the advice from headquarters.

'What's so funny?' asked Mum, looking at him curiously.

'Nothing,' answered Dillon.

Mum was going to question him further, but the surgeon came into the room – Doctor Jason Leang, or Doc J as he'd told Dillon to call him. He had straight black hair with just a few strands of grey, in a neat side part, and wore blue pants and a white shirt. Dillon's eyes were drawn to his striking green bow tie – so bright it almost glowed.

'Good news,' announced Doc J, adjusting his round, wire-rimmed glasses. 'The donor liver is a match. We're going to prep you for surgery right now.'

'Oh, thank goodness!' Mum put a hand to her face. She looked like she was about to burst into tears.

Dillon's stomach clenched. *This is it*, he thought. *It's really going to happen.*

And then his stomach was fine.

And he wondered how he should be feeling.

But at this moment in time, he didn't actually know how to feel.

I should be excited, but I'm not.

I should be scared, but I'm not.

I'm just . . . here!

I think I'm ready!

It was like going out to bat. Anxious until he was actually there.

'Are you okay?' asked Doc J, watching him carefully.

Dillon realised that he probably looked strange just staring and not speaking as he took it all in. 'I'm fine.' Dillon's voice was calm and level. 'It's just been a long wait, and . . . and I think I'm ready for this.'

'That's good,' said Doc J. 'Glad to hear it.'

As the surgeon left the room, Mum jumped up and rummaged in her handbag, pulling out her mobile phone.

'I've got to call your father,' she said, stumbling from the room.

Dillon put his hands behind his head and stared up at the ceiling. His life was about to change. So many things would be different. It wasn't just that he'd no longer need the light box – he'd have more freedom, to go places and do things.

A smile crept onto his face. *I'll need equipment.*

'It turns out that your dad has already booked a flight,' said Mum, coming back into the room. 'He said he had a good feeling about things and that he couldn't wait. He's taking a seven-thirty flight. So he'll be here when you wake up.'

'Can I have a mobile phone?' asked Dillon.

'What?' asked Mum, a little taken aback by the question. 'What brought that on?'

'I'm getting a new liver,' said Dillon. 'One that works. I won't need to sit in a light box anymore. I can go for sleepovers at Jay's house. And I won't need to be half an hour from an airport, either. So I'll be able to go places: school excursions, school camp. And if I'm going to be away from home all the time, I'll need to stay in contact with you, so I can let you know when I'm ready for you to pick me up . . . and stuff.'

'All the time, huh?' Mum laughed. 'I guess you have a lot of catching up to do. You have missed out on so many things.' She looked thoughtful. 'I'll think about it and talk with your dad when he gets here. We'll let you know after the operation.'

'Cool!'

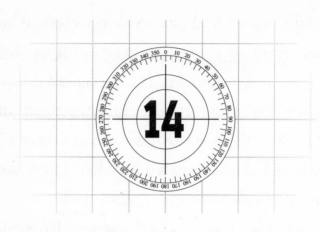

From thereon in, things were a bit of a blur. Dillon could hardly believe it was all actually happening. He had waited for so long. He'd hoped and wished, wondered and imagined, but it had always seemed like such a long way away. It was almost as if it was going to happen to someone else.

But here he was in a hospital bed in

Melbourne. An IV drip was attached to his arm. An anaesthesiologist came to visit, and nurses fussed over him, testing his blood pressure and heart rate. And everyone asked him his name and date of birth, checking it against their forms and the plastic band that had been attached to his wrist.

I guess they want to make sure they put the right organ into the right person, he thought. *Have they ever got it wrong?* But the question just scared him, so he tried to push it away.

And then he was in the operating theatre, everyone gathered around, his mum holding his hand.

'What time is it?' asked Dillon.

'Eight-thirty,' answered Mum. 'Why?'

'Just curious.'

'Strawberry, mint or cola?' asked the anaesthesiologist.

'Huh?' Dillon looked confused.

The anaesthesiologist held up a mask. 'I can put an insert in the anaesthetic mask,' she explained. 'You have a choice of flavours. Or nothing at all, if you'd prefer.'

'Oh,' said Dillon. 'Cola, I suppose.'

Dillon wondered if she had meant smell rather than flavour. And then it suddenly occurred to him that someone must have died in order for him to get his new liver.

He'd always known that would be the case, but this was the first time he had ever really thought about what it meant. It came as a shock. He had spent all this time worrying about his own situation and now he realised that there was someone in a much

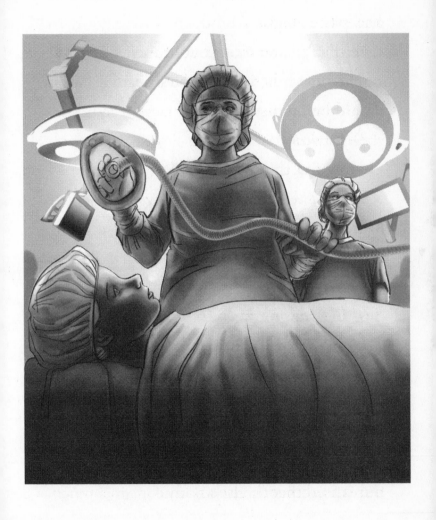

worse position. A real person. Someone who had passed away. And doctors were going to take that person's liver out of their body and put it into his. This person's death is what would be saving his life.

Who was that person?

How did this person die?

Is it a kid like me? Or someone older? Would an older liver last as long as a young one? Would a grown-up liver even fit into my body?

Is it a boy or a girl? Are girl livers the same? Does it make a difference?

Whoever it was would have had family and friends – people upset at their death. He was curious to know how they felt about a part of a person they cared deeply for being put into someone else's body.

His body.

He would have a piece of another person inside of him. In a way, that dead person would live on. Sort of. Through him.

He had a sudden urge to know who that person was.

'Excuse me,' he said to the nurse. 'Who did my liver belong to?'

The nurse looked confused.

'My new liver,' Dillon explained. 'Who did it belong to? What was the person's name?'

'Oh,' said the nurse. 'I don't know.'

'It's against policy to give out any information about the donor,' said Doc J. 'All I can really do is assure you that the liver is healthy and a good match for you.'

Dillon wanted to know why it was against policy, but he didn't get the chance to ask.

'I'm going to put the mask on now,' said the anaesthesiologist. 'Start counting backwards from one hundred and see how far you can get.'

'I'll be right here with you till you're asleep,' said Mum, giving his hand a squeeze. 'And both Dad and I will be waiting for you when you wake up.'

'One hundred. Ninety-nine. Ninety-eight.' Dillon started counting. 'Ninety-seven . . .'

What would happen to his own liver? No one would want it, surely, because it didn't work properly.

'Ninety-six . . .'

Will they throw it out?

'Ninety-five . . .'

He imagined the blood-soaked liver being tossed into a wastepaper basket.

'Ninety-four . . .'

Or maybe I can take it home with me?

'Ninety-four . . .'

He imagined it in a jar, floating in liquid, sitting on his desk at home, where he could watch it while he did his homework every afternoon.

'Ninety-four . . .'

He realised everything was blurry. And all the voices were muffled.

'Ninety-five . . .'

His mouth tasted of cola.

'Ninety . . .'

What number am I up to?

'Nine . . .'

I need to throw up.

That was Dillon's first conscious thought.

He tried to vomit. Nothing came out.

His eyes were closed. He had no real idea of where he was or what was happening. All he knew was that his stomach was churning.

He retched and a thin trickle of

foul-tasting bile escaped, dribbling down his cheek. Someone wiped it away.

He felt hands on his shoulders, leaning him to the side, and something cold and metallic pressed to his cheek.

He retched again. A little more liquid came out.

Dillon was aware of movement and voices around him, but he couldn't open his eyes. He was too tired.

His stomach settled a bit and everything went away.

Until he needed to throw up again.

And again.

And again.

Somewhere, amidst all the spewing, he began to get a sense of where he was and what was going on.

I'm in hospital, aren't I?

I had an operation, didn't I?

I've got a new liver . . . I hope!

He finally opened his eyes. Mum and Dad were there, just like they said they would be. He smiled.

People came and went. Mum and Dad stayed.

He caught a fleeting glimpse of bright green.

Dillon floated in and out of awareness. The only thing he was certain of was that he was thirsty. Scratchy throat, bone-dry mouth, parched thirstiness.

People spoke. He wasn't sure who was talking to whom. To him? To Mum and Dad? To each other?

'Welcome back,' said Mum.

'You're doing well, champ,' said Dad.

'Nausea is quite a common reaction to anaesthetic,' said a nurse.

'It was a textbook operation,' said Doc J.

'I've got flowers here,' said someone.

'I'll get water,' said someone else.

'He's doing well.'

'Nil by mouth for the first twelve hours.'

'It's already after nine pm.'

'It will take some time for the anaesthetic to wear off completely.'

'He'll probably drift in and out of sleep.'

'You don't have to stay here all night.'

'You should get some rest, too.'

'We'd rather wait.'

Dillon heard a mobile ringing. 'Is that my phone?' he whispered.

And then he fell asleep.

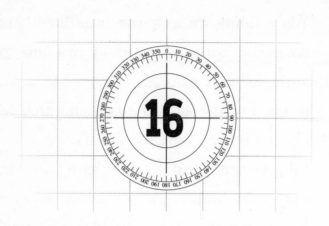

The following morning, Dillon woke properly. His mouth and throat were so dry all he could manage was a hoarse whisper. He was allowed to have a drink of water, and was told that he could have a snack later in the day.

The nurses soon had him propped up and sitting in bed.

'Wow,' said Mum, staring at him, Dad beside her. 'I think you're looking better already. Your skin isn't as yellow.' She came right up to the bed and stared at his face. 'And your eyes . . . they're white.'

A little while later Doc J stopped in to check on him. Dillon noticed that his bow tie was bright orange today. He looked over the charts at the foot of Dillon's bed, where the nurses recorded their obs. He nodded and made 'uh-huh' sounds as he adjusted his glasses. 'I am very pleased with your progress. Everything seems to be going well.'

'You have . . . interesting ties,' said Dillon.

Doc J smiled. 'Bow ties are cool!' He hung the chart back in place and pulled up a seat. 'Right,' he said, looking from Dillon to his parents and back again. 'I'm sure that you're aware of how things will go from here on in. But I'd feel better if I went over it all with you anyway.'

Dillon nodded.

'The transplant was successful,' continued Doc J, 'and there is certainly no sign of rejection. We will, of course, continue to monitor you for the next few days before you are discharged. After which, you will be able to live a fairly normal life, with a couple of provisos. Firstly, you will need to take a daily anti-rejection medication for the rest of your life. I cannot stress how important this is. It is this drug that will ensure your new liver will stay a healthy part of your existing body. It suppresses your immune system so that it doesn't reject the liver.'

'Okay,' said Dillon.

'But it also means you need to be extra careful about infections of any sort. The medication will make it difficult for your body to fight them off. The drug also has some side effects. There is the possibility of kidney damage if you don't stay hydrated. So you must drink plenty of fluids every day. You'll also need to stay out of the sun as much as possible.'

'I think all of that will be a lot easier than the daily light box sessions,' said Mum.

'You bet,' agreed Dillon. 'Way better.'

It occurred to Dillon that he would have to do the opposite to his previous routine. He used to try and be out in the sun as much as possible. Now he would have to limit his exposure. It would take some getting used to.

'Well, I think that's pretty much it,' said Doc J. 'Although I'll endeavour to check in one last time before you're discharged.' He pushed the chair back and shook hands with all three of them in turn.

Dillon noticed his handshake was firm and emphatic. It felt reassuring. It made him feel like everything was going to be great.

'Well,' said Dad, suppressing a laugh, 'no more time travel for you.'

'I beg your pardon?' Doc J stopped in the doorway and looked back.

'Oh, nothing.' Dad laughed. 'It's just a story I used to tell Dillon, while he was in his light box. A little bit of fantasy can make reality bearable.'

'It's not entirely fantasy,' said Doc J.

Now it was Dad's turn to look surprised.

'What do you mean?' asked Dillon, eagerly.

'You *can* time travel,' insisted the surgeon. 'In fact, you are doing it right now. All of us are moving forward into the future. Second by second. Minute by minute. Hour by hour. We can only progress in one direction, of course. And it's rather slow-going. But you do get to see a lot along the way. I've always thought of it as rather exciting.'

He smiled gently and left the room.

'Into the future!' declared Dillon.

Dillon was sitting up in bed writing as Mum entered the room. It had been seven days since his operation.

'Good news,' she said. 'You'll be getting discharged tomorrow morning.'

'That's great,' said Dillon, putting down his pen. 'I am so over this whole hospital thing.'

'Oh, come on,' said Mum. 'It's hasn't been that bad, has it?'

'You mean,' grumbled Dillon, 'apart from the poking and prodding, and the sounds at night that keep me awake, and terrible food with too many soggy vegetables, and that funny smell everywhere ALL the time. And it's boring!'

'Okay, okay,' conceded Mum. 'It's not wonderful. But you've had books and DVDs, an iPod, an iPad *and* a laptop. What more could you want?'

'Friends,' suggested Dillon.

'Yes, all right,' said Mum. 'I see your point. But we're going home tomorrow, and I'm sure your friends will come for a visit.'

Dillon grunted.

'And hasn't Jay been sending you emails?' asked Mum.

'Yeah,' said Dillon glumly, 'but it's not the same as actually having him around.'

'Well, I've got some more news that might cheer you up,' said Mum, looking pleased with herself.

Dillon looked interested.

'You know how you wanted a mobile phone?'

'Yes!' Dillon felt like he was about to jump out of bed with excitement.

'But there will be rules,' insisted Mum. 'I'm not going to have you raking up insane bills. It'll be a pre-paid phone, with twenty dollars of calls per month. You reach the cap and your phone stops working unless you add money to it yourself. Got that?'

'Got it!' Dillon was just happy about finally getting a mobile. He'd work within the limits and then see about getting Mum and Dad to maybe extend them, a little at a time.

'So, what are you doing?' asked Mum, sitting down on the end of his bed.

'Writing a letter,' said Dillon. 'Well . . . trying to anyway.'

'A letter?' asked Mum. 'How very twentieth century of you. Who to?'

'To the family of the donor.' Dillon's face was serious.

'But I thought they couldn't tell you who they are?' said Mum.

'They haven't,' said Dillon. 'And the donor's family aren't given any info about who got the liver, either. But the nurse said

I could write a letter anonymously and that it would get passed on to them.'

'Oh, I see.' Mum smoothed out the bedsheet, the wrinkles suddenly interesting. 'So . . . what have you written?'

'Not much,' admitted Dillon. 'I can't seem to get past thank you. It doesn't seem enough. But I don't know what else to say.'

Mum nodded. 'And they probably wouldn't know what to say to you. Maybe that's why the donor program prefers to keep things anonymous?'

'I guess.' Dillon put the paper and pen aside and picked up his iPad. 'Of course, I might be able to find out who the donor was.'

Mum looked at him with surprise but didn't say anything.

'You can find almost anything with Google.' Dillon held up the iPad and waved it about. 'Entering the date we got the call, with search terms like "liver", "transplant" and "organ donor". Checking online newspapers for accident reports.'

'Are you going to?' asked Mum tentatively.

Dillon shook his head. 'I don't think so.' He dropped the iPad onto the bed. 'If I can't think of what to say in a letter, what's the point in tracking them down?' He shrugged. 'They probably don't even want to hear from me. I might be a horrible reminder that the person they loved is gone.'

Mother and son sat in silence for a while. Dillon traced a finger over the iPad screen.

'You know . . .' His voice trailed away.

'What?' asked Mum, encouragingly.

'Part of me hopes that they'll find me,' he said slowly, not looking up. 'That the donor's family will Google the date and *transplant recipient* and . . . and find me.'

'I think,' said Mum, shifting herself further up the bed so she was beside him, 'that, for now, it's okay if you're just thankful. You have been given a tremendous gift that has come from someone else's tragedy. You don't have to write a letter straight away. Give it some time. After you've adjusted, after you've learned to live a normal life . . . then maybe the words will come. When you're ready.'

'I guess,' said Dillon.

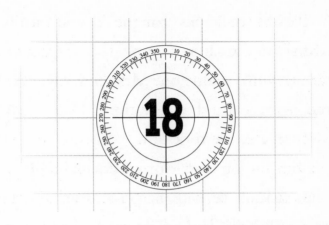

The following day, Dillon was discharged. Dad had already returned home in order to go back to work. But Mum was still with him.

'Am I glad to be getting out of here,' said Dillon, as they waited at the nurses' station. 'Hospitals are sooooooo boring.'

'Yes, yes,' said Mum. 'I know. You've only complained about it a thousand times or so.'

Dillon stuck his tongue out playfully. Mum did the same.

'Sorry to interrupt, Mrs Grayson,' said the nurse behind the station. 'Here is the discharge paperwork.'

Both Dillon and Mum reddened a bit.

As Mum turned her attention to the nurse, Dillon looked around the nurses' station, with its waiting area, which was like a guard post dividing the patient rooms from the outside world. No one in or out without the appropriate forms.

Yep, I'll be glad to get out of here, he thought.

Then he noticed that he was being stared at. Over in the corner of the waiting area were a middle-aged man and woman. They were both watching him.

As he turned to their direction, the man immediately looked away. But the woman continued to watch. She even smiled at him. It was a small, sad smile. A smile that could break your heart.

Dillon noticed that the couple looked tired and haggard – as if they hadn't slept or eaten in days. He wondered if their son or daughter was in one of the rooms, recovering from an operation.

He went over to Mum, who was filling in a form on the counter. 'How long is this going to take?'

'Be patient,' snapped Mum. 'They're not going to let you out of here until all this is done. Leave me be and I'll get it finished a lot quicker.'

Dillon huffed and went to sit down. The couple were watching him again. Dillon smiled and waved. The man's eyes welled up with tears and he clutched a hand to his mouth. The woman touched his arm softly, but it seemed to do little good. He got to his feet, shaking his head. 'I can't do this,' he croaked, and rushed from the room. Dillon thought the woman was about to do something similar, but she took a deep breath and composed herself.

Dillon couldn't seem to look away, even though he felt awkward about watching. It felt like he was intruding on a very private moment.

Slowly, the woman got to her feet and made to follow the man. But part way to the exit she stopped and turned back.

She looked at Dillon again. He saw a resigned determination wash over her face. It was as if she had just come to a decision — an important, life-changing decision.

And then she was walking towards him.

'Hello,' she said in a raspy voice. She cleared her throat and continued. 'You're Dillon, aren't you?'

'Yes,' said Dillon, puzzled by how she knew.

'I . . . I . . .' She hesitated. 'I just wanted to meet you. To see . . . to see what you were like.' She reached out a hand and rested it on his cheek. Dillon could feel the trembling of her fingers. 'You seem like a nice boy.'

She took her hand back and turned to go, then stopped again. She turned back to look at him one last time, with eyes so sad they could have drowned a city in tears. 'I am very glad that your operation was a success.'

Dillon's eyes widened. He suddenly recognised the sadness in the woman's eyes. It was the same sadness he had seen at the funeral when his grandfather had died. It was grief!

As the woman made her way to the door, Dillon knew who she must be. And that she had found him.

'Wait!' he called after her.

The nurse glared at him disapprovingly. Mum turned to stare at him questioningly. The woman stopped in the doorway but didn't look back.

Dillon hesitated, his throat tightening, his mind uncertain.

'Thank you,' he finally said. 'Thank you so much.'

The woman nodded and rushed out.

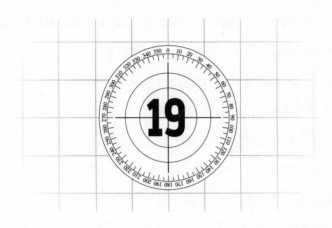

Dillon surges forward through time.
  Seconds, minutes and hours pass.
  Days, months and years . . .
  Sixteen years into the future.

It is midnight . . . on the dot. Magic hour. That time of night when anything might happen.

A young girl is strapped down onto a stretcher. Tubes and wires are connecting her to plastic bags and monitors. There are dried tears in the corners of her eyes.

Machinery whirr into action and the stretcher is lifted into the air. Up into the belly of the waiting aircraft.

Inside, the nurse secures the stretcher to the wall and starts doing obs.

The girl begins to cry again.

The nurse attempts to calm her down. He tells the girl that her mother is on the way – that she'll be here soon and that she'll be on the plane to Melbourne with her.

The girl nods her understanding, but continues to quietly sob.

The pilot comes out of the cockpit, has a word to the nurse, then approaches the girl.

He is tall, with close-cropped blond hair and a fair complexion. He has a friendly smile and welcoming eyes.

'Hey there,' he says to the girl. 'I'm told you're going to Melbourne for a special operation. A transplant.'

The girl nods shakily.

'Guess what?' continues the pilot. 'I know how you feel. Really. You know why?'

The girl shakes her head, intrigued. She has stopped crying.

'Because, sixteen years ago, when I was eleven years old, I was in your place,' he says. 'I was rushed onto an RFDS plane like this and flown to Melbourne so that doctors could put a new liver into my body.'

The girl's eyes are wide with wonder.

'What's your name?' he asks.

'Jade.' The girl's voice is tiny and tremulous.

The pilot extends a hand. He gently takes hers and shakes it. 'Pleased to meet you, Jade,' he says. 'My name is Dillon and I'll be your pilot today. And I promise to get you safely to Melbourne.'

A BRIEF HISTORY OF THE RFDS

The Royal Flying Doctor Service of Australia (RFDS) began as the dream of the Reverend John Flynn, a minister with the Presbyterian Church. He witnessed the struggle of pioneers living in remote areas with no available medical care. Flynn's vision was to provide a 'mantle of safety' for these people, and on 15 May 1928 his dream became a reality with the opening of the Australian Inland Mission Aerial Medical Service (later renamed the Royal Flying Doctor Service) in Cloncurry, Queensland.

Over the next few years, the Service began to expand across the country, and by the 1950s was acknowledged by former Prime Minister Sir Robert Menzies as 'perhaps the single greatest contribution to the effective settlement of the far distant country that we have witnessed in our time'.

Until the 1960s, the RFDS rarely owned its own aircraft. Progressively, the RFDS began to purchase its own aircraft and employ dedicated pilots and engineers.

Today, the Royal Flying Doctor Service is one of the largest and most comprehensive aeromedical organisations in the world. Using the latest in aviation, medical and communications technology, it delivers extensive health care and 24-hour emergency service to those who live, work and travel throughout Australia. The RFDS has a fleet of 66 aircraft operating from 23 bases located across the nation and provides medical assistance to over 290,000 people every year.

Did you know? The Royal Flying Doctor Service was granted use of the 'Royal' prefix in 1955 after a visit from Queen Elizabeth II!

Royal Flying Doctor Service
The furthest corner. The finest care.

REAL-LIFE MIDNIGHT FLIGHT

This story was inspired by the real-life experience of RFDS patient Brendan Wells. Brendan was born with Crigler-Najjar Syndrome, a rare genetic disorder that meant his liver was unable to process and remove bilirubin. The toxic chemical is a by-product created by the body during the natural breakdown of red blood cells. To reduce the amount of bilirubin in his bloodstream and control the severe jaundice that it caused, Brendan spent about six hours every day sitting in an ultraviolet light box.

All that changed in 2010, when he was flown to Melbourne in the middle of the night by the RFDS for a liver transplant. While Brendan's illness was uncommon, the evacuation was routine for RFDS Central Operations, which makes at least one interstate flight per week for Adelaide residents requiring life-saving or specialist surgery at an interstate hospital – day or night.

Brendan made a rapid recovery after his surgery, and now has the freedom to travel. 'A couple of years ago that was completely out of the question,' said his father, Tim. His school's Year 7 camping trip to Kangaroo Island was completely off the agenda, and even Christmas holidays visiting relatives at Port Pirie were difficult. Tim would have had to spend half a day dismantling the light box to take it with them, and the transplant team at the Royal Children's Hospital in Melbourne had to know their every move in case a liver became available. Ideally, Brendan was meant to be no more than thirty minutes from Adelaide Airport so he could be flown out quickly.

Life today is not without its complications. The seventeen-year-old must take an anti-rejection drug every twelve hours for the rest of his life. It suppresses Brendan's immune system, so he has to be very conscious of avoiding infection. Side effects from the drug also mean that he has to stay out of the sun and drink plenty of fluids to limit kidney damage. But, as Brendan says, 'I don't have to go under the lights anymore.

And I don't have to worry about people at school asking, "Why are you yellow?", which they did a lot.'

'Brendan knows the gift he has been given and he is highly respectful of the opportunity,' Tim said. 'It is why we are very happy to promote the "Flying Doctor" and organ donation. Your money goes where it is needed, and it makes a difference. Brendan has the scar to prove it.'

PATIENT TRANSFERS

Whether it is transporting patients from hospital to hospital, by air or by road, the RFDS play a vital role in inter-hospital transfers of patients in less urgent cases in many parts of Australia. This particularly includes transferring patients from small hospitals in rural and remote areas to larger hospitals in regional centres or metropolitan areas, where more specialist services are available.

Every day RFDS Central Operations (SA/NT) conducts an average of twenty inter-hospital transfers of patients from a country hospital to a major metropolitan hospital for life-saving treatment or a higher level of care. Once a patient is admitted to a country hospital, often their condition can deteriorate or tests reveal an urgent need for specialist treatment at a major hospital.

Urgent transfers can sometimes involve organ transplant patients or a newborn baby requiring heart surgery interstate. Inter-hospital transfers are not just for people living in the country – 1 in every 20 people transferred has an Adelaide postcode. In 2014–15, RFDS Central Operations conducted 6857 inter-hospital transfers throughout South and Central Australia.

Across Australia in 2014–15, the RFDS performed 59,596 inter-hospital transfers in addition to 4336 aeromedical emergency evacuations, 332 patients transferred from clinics, and 409 repatriations.

PHONETIC ALPHABET

During times of difficult communication the phonetic alphabet is of great use. 'S' and 'F' can sound the same, as can 'D' and 'B'. Spelling of names is sometimes required. For example, 'Smith' is transmitted as Sierra Mike India Tango Hotel using the phonetic alphabet.

LETTER	PHONETIC	SPOKEN AS
A	ALPHA	AL FAH
B	BRAVO	BRAH VO
C	CHARLIE	CHAR LEE
D	DELTA	DELLTA

LETTER	PHONETIC	SPOKEN AS
E	ECHO	ECK OH
F	FOXTROT	FOKS TROT
G	GOLF	GOLF
H	HOTEL	HOH TEL
I	INDIA	IN DEE AH
J	JULIET	JEW LEE ETT
K	KILO	KEY LOH
L	LIMA	LEE MAH
M	MIKE	MIKE
N	NOVEMBER	NO VEMBER
O	OSCAR	OSS CAH
P	PAPA	PAH PAH
Q	QUEBEC	KEH BECK
R	ROMEO	ROH ME OH
S	SIERRA	SEE AIR RAH
T	TANGO	TANG GO
U	UNIFORM	YOU NEE FORM
V	VICTOR	VICK TAH
W	WHISKEY	WISS KEY
X	X-RAY	ECKS RAY
Y	YANKEE	YANG KEY
Z	ZULU	ZOO LOO

Missed out on *Royal Flying Doctor Service: Remote Rescue*? Read on for an extract!

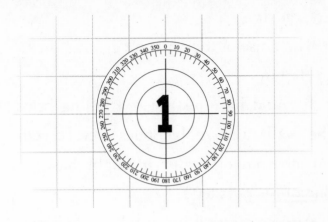

Dawson crept along, heart pounding in his chest. He trod carefully, quietly, his eyes searching the nooks and crannies.

He stepped over rubble and out through the door in the crumbling wall. The sun hit him in the eyes, dazzling him. Squinting, he raised a hand to shield his face.

Crack!

The noise of rock hitting against rock.

He ran.

It could have just been a falling brick – the walls and rubble piles were certainly unstable enough. But it might have been one of his pursuers.

And he didn't want to take a chance.

Dawson skirted the old building. His runners sank into the sand baked by the harsh sun.

He stopped at the edge of the wall and peered into the main street. There were people near a bright red car at the very far end of the dirt and gravel road. But, otherwise, there was no one else close by. He took a deep breath, then dashed across the street.

Breathing hard, legs pumping, he made it through to the next ageing building. He surveyed his surroundings.

Streaks of sunlight hit the tired walls, making the shadows seem even darker. Dawson peered into the gloomy corners, looking for movement . . . for signs of life. Nothing.

He inched forward, back pressed up against the wall.

He looked into the first room. Reasonably intact, it had four almost complete walls; even the window frame was still in place. But the room was filled with debris, where the roof had caved in.

Dawson moved on.

The next room by contrast was barely there. The wall with the doorway was the only one completely standing. Dawson continued a little quicker.

Another room and he was at the back doorway. Like the front room, it still had its wooden frame but no actual door. He looked out cautiously before stepping forward.

'Boo!'

Dawson jumped, stumbled and fell onto the pile of nearby bricks, scraping his knee.

A young girl giggled, ran past him in a flash of pink and disappeared around the corner.

Dawson sighed. This was silly. Why was he scared? It was just a dumb game of hide and seek or chasey or whatever it was.

Then again, it might have something to

do with the fact that he was creeping around an almost deserted ghost town – a *real live* ghost town. *Or should that be a real* dead *ghost town*, he wondered.

'Yo, kids!' he heard Dad's voice echo around the bricks. 'Front and centre.'

Dawson picked himself up and dusted off his grimy blue shorts and t-shirt. He clambered up the pile of bricks and looked for signs of his siblings.

Nothing. They were better at games than he was.

Dawson yelped as he slipped down the bricks, landing hard at the bottom. He sighed again. Why had he agreed to play?

He got up and walked through the dilapidated building, along the neat little path out the front and past the sign saying

'Exchange Hotel'. Low ropes strung between short wooden posts marked out the boundaries of the building.

Dawson looked back at the partially collapsed hotel. The sun was going down behind it, shining through the glassless windows, empty doorways and crumbling brickwork, making it glow. It almost looked beautiful . . . in a weird sort of way.

'Kids!'

Dad was at the end of the main road, at the crossroads on the edge of Farina, the small abandoned town that they were visiting. As usual, Dad wore blue jeans and a white t-shirt. He *always* wore jeans, even if he was going out to a fancy dinner. Mum would wear a nice dress and Dad would wear a shirt, tie and suit jacket – with daggy blue jeans. Not a good look. Dawson thought jeans were a silly thing to wear on their holiday, given the heat.

'Coming!' He waved to Dad and started walking. To his left he could see his little sister, Emma, spring out from the building next to the hotel and race to Dad, skipping over debris.

Glancing the other way, he saw his older sister, Samantha, climbing out of a rusted old car shell.

How did she get all the way up there?

He shook his head. She must have climbed through the car's window to get inside. He had looked at the automobile when they'd first arrived and its doors were rusted shut. There were lots of sharp edges on it. She could have cut herself. Not for the first time, he marvelled at her reckless behaviour.

'What happened, son?' asked Dad, pointing to Dawson's knee, where a small trickle of blood was already drying.

'I scared him,' said Emma, proudly. 'And he fell over.'

'No, you didn't,' protested Dawson. 'I was just startled, that's all.'

'I scared you,' repeated Emma, grinning broadly.

'Ha,' Samantha mocked as she jogged over. 'Is poor little Dawsy-Wawsy spooked by the ghost town?'

'Hey,' interrupted Dad, 'enough of that! I thought I told you guys to be careful. It's so easy to get hurt in amongst all the rubble and broken building bits.'

Dawson smiled. *Broken building bits.* Alliteration. Ever since he'd learned the term at school, he'd noticed how often Dad used it, stringing together words starting with the same letter. 'Vile voluminous vomit.' Those had been Dad's most used words when Emma had gastro a few months ago. He glanced at Samantha. She looked back, trying to keep a straight face. And then they both burst out laughing. It was an ongoing joke between them.

'Oi,' said Dad. 'This is no laughing matter. If you get hurt, there's no doctor around. All we've got is a first-aid kit.' His hands were on his hips now as he slipped into full-on Dad Mode. 'And if you get seriously injured, what then? Do you see a hospital nearby? Huh?'

The kids looked blankly at each other and then back to Dad.

'No! Of course not,' continued Dad. 'We'd need to find some way of contacting the RFDS.'

'R . . . F . . . D . . . what?' asked Emma.

'RFDS,' said Dad, smiling now. 'The Royal Flying Doctor Service. They're doctors and nurses who fly around in planes to help people in the middle of nowhere.'

'Wow,' breathed Em. 'Doctors who fly.'

Dad turned his attention to Dawson's bloodied knee. 'You need a bandaid for that?'

'Nah,' answered Dawson. 'It's just a scratch.'

'Anyway,' continued Dad, 'no running around in the collapsed buildings. It's dangerous. Got that?'

'Sure,' Samantha said, a gleam in her eyes.

Emma nodded.

'Besides which, if you're running around you're not looking at the sights properly. And there's so much to take in . . .' He turned around. 'But we'll see more of it tomorrow. Come on. We better get back to camp and start dinner.'

As he headed along the dirt road, Dawson looked back at the town of Farina. It was a ghost town. But that didn't mean it was full of ghosts. Farina was abandoned. No one lived there and it was literally falling apart.

Bathed in the golden light of sunset, the place did look supernatural. Dawson imagined spirits of the past hiding in the buildings and pacing the deserted streets.

He remembered the *Ghastly Ghosts* video game he liked so much. There was a deserted town in that. All he needed now was an ecto-blaster to hunt ghosts with. He smiled. Ghostly video game images floated through Dawson's mind as he turned and followed his family.

Dinner was baked beans on fried bread. Dawson was sick of camp food. Dad wasn't a great cook at home, but his camping menu was even worse. You'd think that as a stay-at-home dad, he'd be able to cook better. Sadly not.

If they camped anywhere near shops, they had sausages in bread. If not, then whatever they ate came out of a tin. The bread was fried because it had gone stale in the heat.

'You can revive anything by frying it in butter.' This was Dad's cooking motto. Dawson wasn't so sure about it. He imagined buttery bush ants and witchetty grubs popping and splattering in a frying pan. He grimaced. But he was hungry, so he shovelled beans and butter-sodden bread into his mouth.

Dawson looked around as he chewed. The campground was nestled in amongst a scattering of trees, about a five-minute walk from the town itself. The glow of their lantern lit up their immediate area. In the distance was another circle of light. Campers who had recently arrived – probably the same people who'd been hanging around earlier, judging by the red car.

'What are we doing tomorrow?' asked Samantha.

'I reckon we can spend a little over half a day here,' said Dad. 'We'll have a late lunch and then get moving. It's about fifty-five kilometres to Marree, which is our next stop.'

'Is that another spooky town?' mumbled Emma, her mouth full of beans.

'You mean *ghost* town,' Samantha corrected.

'Nah,' said Dad. 'Marree is an ordinary town – people still live in it. Nothing special, though. It's just a place to camp before we move on to Oodnadatta.' He scooped the last of his food into his mouth but continued talking, spitting little bits of food in his excitement. 'There's lots to see before we go. Aside from the buildings of the town itself, there's bits of the Old Ghan railway, some carriages, water towers and other stuff to the east. Then there's the cemetery . . .'

Dad was now in full-on Dad Tourist Mode. He loved adventure and seeing things. He was always bursting with stories of overseas travel that he and Mum had done before they had kids. This trip, driving to Uluru and back, was supposed to be a test. The first big holiday the whole family did together, now that Emma was old enough. And if things worked out, they would consider an overseas trip the following year.

But things hadn't quite worked out. Mum hadn't been able to come with them. She was stuck back in Adelaide, finishing off a case. She was a lawyer, and the company she worked for needed her to stay an extra week. So the rest of the family had started the trip without her. She intended to fly to Uluru later and meet them there, then they would do the trip back by car.

As Dad droned on about the history of Farina and what they would see in the morning, Dawson's thoughts drifted to his family, the Millers. They were a bit annoying, but not too bad. He guessed that he loved them, even though they drove him crazy sometimes.

Samantha was his older sister. She was twelve.

Sam loved exploring, so Dawson knew this trip was right up her alley. She was adventurous and daring. Dawson admired the way she just did things, no matter what anybody else said . . . but it also scared him a little. He sometimes wished he could be a bit more like her.

Emma was his younger sister. She was seven.

Everyone loved Em. She was cheeky but cute, mischievous but kind, and the baby of the family. She often made Dawson laugh – even when she was being irritating. For her, everything was a game. No wonder she was so good at hide and seek.

At almost eleven, Dawson was stuck in the middle. Em and Sam always called him Daws. But Em, with her little-kid way of saying things very carefully, made it sound like 'Doors'. Dad always called him 'son', almost like an acknowledgement that he was a boy trapped between two sisters.

Dawson sighed. His sisters were enjoying this camping holiday more than he was. He didn't mind camping usually, but the thought of doing it all the way to Uluru and back didn't thrill him. Especially since they had to pack and unpack every day or two.

He would have liked it better if Mum was with them. Dad was a bit intense with the touristy stuff, wanting to stop and examine absolutely everything. ('Look, there's a historic building.' 'Look, there's a cultural landmark.' 'Look, there's a brick that might have been part of an important structure a century ago.') Mum was more reasonable. A bit touristy, yeah, but in a fun way.

Dawson also missed his Xbox. Not that he would admit it. Dad was always going on about how he spent too much time playing video games.

Dawson tuned back into the conversation. Dad was now prattling on about the animals they'd seen so far and others they might encounter on their trip – kangaroos, emus, lizards, echidnas and something called a thorny devil.

'Hey,' said Dad. 'What's the collective noun for a group of emus?'

'Herd,' said Sam.

'Flock,' said Dawson, looking at his sister as if she knew nothing. 'They're birds.'

'Nope,' said Dad.

Sam poked her tongue out at Dawson.

'Crowd?' said Em, hopefully.

Sam laughed.

'Actually,' said Dad. 'That's pretty close.'

Em smiled proudly.

'It's a *mob* of emus,' Dad finally revealed.

Em giggled and Dawson smiled at her.

'A marauding mob of elegant emus.' Dad was putting on his radio announcer's voice, while extending his neck back and forth with a strange movement that he obviously thought made him resemble an emu. He was wrong. It just looked silly. 'Casually cruising for cacti across the desolate desert.'

Em laughed. Sam groaned. Dawson rolled his eyes.

'Righty-oh,' said Dad with a chuckle. 'Enough animal alliteration. Time we all turned in. The sun will have us up bright and early tomorrow morning.'

Sam stared into the gloom. The moon cast eerie shadows across the canvas. Quietly, she climbed out of her sleeping bag and tiptoed past Em, who slept soundly, clutching her fluffy pink bunny. She carefully unzipped the tent, hoping the sound wouldn't wake Dawson, who shared the tent's other room with Dad.

There was no danger of disturbing Dad, who could sleep through an earthquake, but Dawson was another matter. He was a light sleeper and if he discovered her, he might follow and lecture her about how she shouldn't be sneaking out of the tent at night. Or he might even tell Dad. Dawson could be a bit of a spoilsport sometimes.

Sam often thought that Dawson didn't behave like a ten-year-old should. He was always trying to be so grown-up. Of course, his answer to that would be to remind her that he wasn't a ten-year-old – he was an *almost*-eleven-year-old. Sam nearly laughed out loud.

Slipping on her shoes, she crept out and zipped the tent up again. She paused for a moment to listen. All quiet in the tent. She smiled to herself and moved off.

The night was chilly and she wrapped her arms around herself as she walked in her shorts and t-shirt along the road to Farina.

She did this in every place they camped. Waiting until the others were asleep, she would sneak out for a private midnight wander. It was her chance for a bit of alone-time and an opportunity to explore. And the lure of a dead-of-night visit to a ghost town was too enticing to pass up.

Reaching the edge of the town, she stopped to gaze at the moon-bathed buildings and streets. In the darkness, Sam could imagine the buildings were not falling apart, that they might have people sleeping in them. And in the surrounding night might be . . . anything. People. More buildings. A city. What had seemed lonely and desolate and abandoned by day was mysterious and full of potential by night.

Sam breathed in deeply the evening air, smiled and took off down the main street at a sprint.

Yes, she was tired. Yes, she would be woken early by the rising sun (or maybe even earlier by her sister). But for a few minutes at least, before she headed back to bed, this town was all hers.

An **RFDS** Adventure

REMOTE RESCUE

GEORGE IVANOFF

OUT NOW

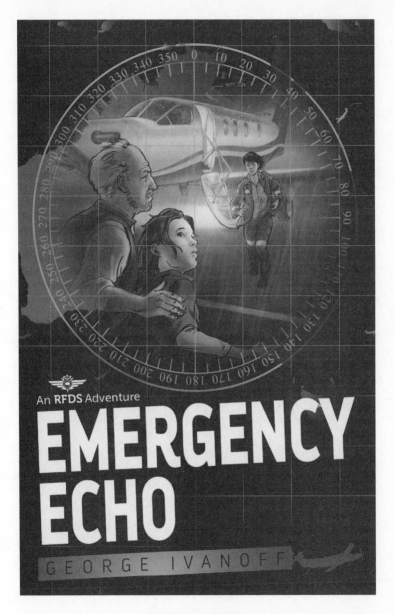

An **RFDS** Adventure

EMERGENCY ECHO

GEORGE IVANOFF

OUT NOW

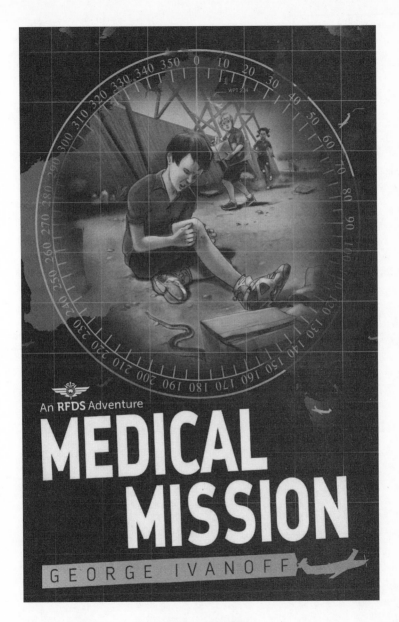

An RFDS Adventure

MEDICAL MISSION

GEORGE IVANOFF

OUT NOW